THE
MAGIC
ROOM

THE MAGIC ROOM

Story by SCOTT SPENCER
Pictures by COCO DUPUY

 Harmony Books | New York

For Celeste and Asher

Did you ever hear what happened to Phoebe? It happened when she was just about your age. Phoebe, you see, was brave and smart. And funny. Very funny. Her problem was that her mother and father didn't know how brave, smart, and funny she was.

Her parents were very busy people. They worked all day. And that wasn't all. They also had a secret room where they worked all night. They called themselves Scientists, but if you asked Phoebe she would have told you they were Magicians.

One night, after Dad tucked her into bed and gave her a kiss on the forehead and Mom came in to tell her a story, after the lights in her room were out and the door was closed, Phoebe just couldn't stand it anymore. She had to see what was in that room. And so she crept out of bed. She put on a mask and tiptoed down the hall.

Oh, down the hall, down the hall, down the long and narrow hall. And at the end of her walk there was the door. Usually the door was closed tight tight tight, but tonight they'd forgotten to close it all the way. Phoebe saw the light in the crack. And she pushed her way in—just as quietly as she could.

Mom and Dad were so busy, they didn't even notice. Phoebe hid herself behind a giant rabbit and had herself a nice long look around. And what sights there were! First there was Mom and Dad, all dressed in white. And all around the room—the most amazing things Phoebe had ever seen. A horse as puny as a peach. A rabbit as big as a refrigerator. A

rain cloud right there in the room, raining away. A pea as big as your head. Just look around for yourself and see what I mean.

Was Phoebe scared? A little. But more than anything else, she was excited. Here at last was a game they *all* could play. And she was so excited—she forgot to hide. "Mom! Dad!" she called out. "This is so great! I'm going to call this the Magic Room!"

Were they happy to see her? Oh, I wish I could say they were. But they turned around and saw Phoebe on top of the rabbit and their faces looked very, very cross indeed. "We told you never to come into this room," Mom said. "You march with me," said Dad. And he took Phoebe by her arm.

Down the hall, down the hall, down the long and narrow hall. And right back into bed.

"Now you stay here," Dad said, putting Phoebe in her bed. "I don't want to hear a sound, and I don't want you up and around."

"You made a rhyme," said Phoebe, in a tiny voice. "Sound and around." She was still hoping, you see, that Dad might play. But he just shook his head and put his finger on his lips, as if to say husshhh, and then he backed out the door.

Did Phoebe fall right back to sleep? I wish I could say she did. But she was far too angry for sleep. She simply lay there and had rotten thoughts. She thought about all the times she wanted to play with Mom and Dad and they said no because they were...too busy! Too busy to play dress-up. Too busy to—

But wait!!! Just then Phoebe heard the most frightening, dreadful, tremendous, screaming BOOOOM. And then it was quiet again. It was quieter than a mouse blinking.

Phoebe called out in a rather polite voice. "Oh, Mom? Daddy?" She waited for an answer—but when she heard none she got out of bed. After all, you can't hear a sound like that and just do *nothing*. Maybe something was wrong. Maybe they *needed* her.

So Phoebe ran from her room. She was a good runner. And she ran down the hall. She could see—way, way down the hall—the Magic Room. The door was wide open, and smoke was coming out of it. Lots of smoke. Oh, and I almost forgot to tell you: The smoke was *purple*.

Phoebe stood at the door to the Magic Room and waited for the smoke to clear. Then she heard a sound. She heard, Cough Cough. But it didn't sound like her mother or father coughing. It sounded like someone very very small. An elf maybe. Or a fish. No, wait. Fish don't cough. Then she heard it again. Cough Cough. She wanted to go in and see—but she remembered what her parents had said. She wasn't allowed.

Then she heard someone say, "Phoebe? Is that you?" It sounded like Dad's voice. Only tiny.

"Phoebe!" said another voice, and this one sounded like Mom. "Phoebe," the Mom-ish voice said, "we don't want you to come in here."

What should she do? She didn't want to disobey, but it was as plain as the nose on her face that they were in trouble. And they needed her.

And so Phoebe walked into the Magic Room. It was kind of a wreck after the big explosion. There was a hole in the wall and another in the ceiling. She saw the moon looking right down through it. And then Phoebe saw something that I don't think any child has seen before. She saw her parents, her own mother and her dear father. And they looked exactly like themselves, with the same kind of eyes and the same kind of hair, and the same kind of clothes, and the same kind of shoes. They looked the way they always looked, except for one thing: They were four inches tall.

Do you know how little that is? Four inches is how long it is from the top of your nose to the tip of your chin. Four inches is how long a mouse is. A piece of broccoli is bigger than four inches. Can you imagine what it would be like if your parents were smaller than broccoli?

Phoebe lifted her parents and put them in her hand. They looked at her and she looked at them. This was quite an unusual situation, and they all had a lot of quick thinking to do. Could they still tell her what to do? Could they still tell her to go to bed and say that they wouldn't play with her anymore? Now that they were the size of teeny-tiny dolls, couldn't she play with them whenever she wanted?

I wonder what you would do if your parents were four inches tall and standing in a room filled with purple smoke. I bet you would do just what Phoebe did. She stuck her little parents in the pocket of her pajamas and quick as she could she ran to safety.

When they reached the kitchen, Phoebe set them down on the table. They were awfully upset. They really didn't want to be so very small. "What will become of us?" they cried. "How can we drive our car? How can we go to work? We can't even turn the pages of our books with no pictures!"

"Don't worry," said Phoebe. "I will take care of you."

Just think of all the good ideas you have had but no one would listen because you were too small. But now, Phoebe wasn't small anymore. In fact, next to her parents she was a giant. "What you two need is some raspberry ice cream," she said. And with that, she skipped down the hall and came back with two tiny bowls and two tiny spoons. I suppose you've already guessed where she got them. That's right—from her dollhouse!

When Mom and Dad had finished their ice cream, Phoebe took a wet paper towel and wiped their faces. When your mouth is so small, it is difficult not to get a little mess on your face while eating. "Did you enjoy your ice cream?" she asked them. They both said they had, and when Phoebe put them back into her pocket, it seemed that they weighed a little more than they had before.

"Now we are going to have some great good times together," said Phoebe, skipping down the hall.

"Where are you taking us?" her parents called. Their little hands held on to the top of her pocket so they could see out. Phoebe was bringing them to her bedroom, where she kept her toys and where day after day she had played all alone.

She placed her parents in the dollhouse. They looked like they really belonged there. Then, she put a terrific black bat mask on her father, and for her mother she chose something very special indeed—an Indian headdress that had come with her Hiawatha doll. Mom and Dad looked so unbelievably cute. It really gave Phoebe a nice warm feeling in her heart to see them so.

"Just look at yourselves," Phoebe said, placing a mirror before them.

Dad crept up to the mirror and looked at himself. He did look awfully silly in that bat mask, and he was so surprised that he laughed. Oh, it wasn't a big, roaring, falling-down-and-holding-your-sides laugh. But it *was* a laugh. And do you know what happened when he laughed? The mask popped right off. And do you know *why* it popped off? Because suddenly Dad's head was too big for the mask.

"I think I just grew," Dad said.

Then it was Mom's turn to look in the mirror. She looked like a bird in her brightly colored feathers, and when she saw her reflection she laughed too. She had such a nice laugh. And when she laughed the headdress snapped and flew right off. It no longer fit. "I think I just grew too," Mom said, touching her head where the headdress had been.

They were growing. And though they were still very small, there was no doubt that they were no longer just four inches tall. They seemed perhaps six inches tall now. The size of asparagus. Or half a ruler.

"I think looking in the mirror makes us grow," said Phoebe's father.

"Oh no, no," disagreed Phoebe's mother. "I don't think it's the mirror that makes us grow. I think it's the feathers or the mask."

Her parents were Scientists and they liked to figure things out. And they were good at it, too. But this time they weren't coming up with the right answer.

Phoebe knew the secret. She knew why they were growing. She reached down and picked them up. "Want to grow some more?" she asked.

"Oh yes, yes, yes," they both said, their little eyes sparkling.

And so Phoebe put her parents in her toy Ferris wheel and gave it a good hard spin. Around and around and around they went, and they laughed so loudly that they sounded like children. And then—crash and smash—the Ferris wheel broke into a million pieces. Her parents had grown again and they had crushed it all to bits.

They picked themselves up and shook the Ferris wheel dust off their clothes. "We grew again!" they shouted with glee. "What is this magical science that makes us grow?"

"If you can't guess, I won't tell you," said Phoebe, as she tickled them under their little arms, and their perky little chins. By the time she was finished they were laughing so hard their faces were red as radishes. And they had grown until they almost came up to Phoebe's waist.

"Oh wonderful, wonderful," Phoebe's father said, panting.

"Wait," said Phoebe's mother, wiping away a tear of laughter. "We have to figure out why this is happening." She looked around the room, searching for clues.

"Perhaps the spinning motion made us grow," said Phoebe's thoughtful father.

But Phoebe would have none of it, and though she knew it was not polite to interrupt her parents when they were having one of their important discussions, she knew that tonight was a special occasion.

"Knock, knock," said Phoebe.

"Who's there?" asked her mother.

"Ach," said Phoebe.

"Ach who?" said her father.

"Aw, you got a cold?" said Phoebe. And they all burst out with wild laughter. And clapped their hands. And grew another inch.

Phoebe was so happy that they were laughing at her jokes and games. I think it was the happiest night of her life. She gathered her parents into her arms and hugged them. But they were far too excited for that, and soon they were on the bed, jumping up and down and breaking all the rules. "Whee!" she cried. "Whee!" her parents cried along with her.

Phoebe sat them down very carefully on the edge of the bed and commenced to do her most wonderful dances for them. Her dances were part ballet, part gymnastics, part karate, part rock 'n' roll, and part just crazy jumping up and down. Usually her dances made her parents say "calm down," but tonight Mom and Dad watched her and laughed. And the more they laughed, the more they grew.

"She's saving us," Dad said to Mom.

"Oh I know, I know," said Mom, but she could barely say it, so hard was she laughing.

"The more we laugh," said Dad.

"The more we grow," said Mom, finishing his thought for him.

"Watch!" said Phoebe. And she stood on her head. Her pajama top fell over her face, and a moment later Phoebe hit the floor with a thud.

"Hurrah, hurrah!" her parents cheered. And now they had grown so much, they were just Phoebe's size.

"Would you like to stop here?" asked Phoebe. "That way we can all be the same size and play forever."

"Oh no, we mustn't," said her parents.

But she could tell by their voices that a part of them would have been very satisfied indeed to remain just her size.

"Laugh us up to our old sizes again," said her father, with a little shrug of regret.

"Well then, OK," said Phoebe. "Listen to this." She turned for a moment so all they could see was her back. And then she leaped into the air and faced them again—singing.

> I know things that
> You don't even know I know.
> I feel things that would make you
> So surprised.
> Listen to what I say!
> Watch the things I do!
> And I'll be oh so happy
> And I will shine for you.
>
> Let's hold back the night
> With the sound of ho ho ho
> Let's hold each other tight
> And never ever let go
> Listen to what I say!
> Watch the things I do!
> And I'll be oh so happy
> And I will shine for you.

And then Phoebe pointed at her parents and said, "Everybody—SING!" And with that joyous yell, the three of them opened their mouths and began to sing.

And as they sang, they grew. And grew. And grew. The laughter was magic, but the song was a *miracle*. Do you know what I mean by a miracle? It is like a wish come true, but a wish so huge and special you didn't even dare to wish it.

Phoebe's parents sang the whole song, and when they were at the end of it, when the song was all gone, they were right back to the same size they had been before the big explosion in the Magic Room.

But do you know what was the most wonderful part of all? (At least I think so.) Even though they were large again, Phoebe's parents did not stop singing and laughing. Maybe they enjoyed being so happy and never wanted it to stop. Or maybe they were afraid that if they got gloomy again they would go back to being small.

And so, that night, though it was past bedtime, all the lights shined in the windows of Phoebe's house and the sounds of laughter and singing could be heard. It was one happy house. Even the smoke danced out of the chimney.

It wasn't all that long before Phoebe's parents were back at work in the Magic Room again. The horse was back, and so was the rabbit. And even though they still did most of their work by themselves, they no longer locked the door. They had a helper in the Magic Room sometimes—someone just about your age. And I bet you can guess who their new helper was.

Published by Harmony Books, a division of Crown Publishers, Inc.,
225 Park Avenue South, New York, New York 10003
and represented in Canada by the Canadian MANDA Group
HARMONY and colophon are trademarks of Crown Publishers, Inc.
Manufactured in Japan

Library of Congress Cataloging-in-Publication Data

Spencer, Scott.
The magic room.
Summary: Phoebe's parents, who are magicians, forbid her to enter the magic room
where they work, until an accident shrinks them to tiny size
and they need her help in returning to normal.
[1. Magicians—Fiction. 2. Magic—Fiction.
3. Size—Fiction] I. Dupuy, C. J., ill. II. Title.
PZ7.S74826Mag   1986   [Fic]   86-18348

ISBN 0-517-56451-3
10 9 8 7 6 5 4 3 2 1